Visit us on the Web at www.clavis-publishing.com.

Miles Won't Smile written by Jackie Azúa Kramer and illustrated by Martina Schachenhuber

ISBN 978-1-60537-692-9

This book was printed in April 2021 at Nikara, M. R. Štefánika 858/25, 963 01 Krupina, Slovakia.

First Edition
10 9 8 7 6 5 4 3 2 1

MILES
won't
SMILE

written by
Jackie Azúa Kramer

Clavis
NEW YORK

illustrated by
Martina Schachenhuber

Daisy is thrilled to be a big sister and is knee deep
in toys for her little brother, Miles.

Miles can play with Mr. Rabbit or my doll with long hair, she thinks.
He can build and stack with these blocks or draw pictures with my crayons.

Daisy scoops up the toys
and drops them in Miles' crib.

Surprise!

Daisy cheers when Dad and Miles
enter the room.

"Thank you, Daisy," says Dad.
"But, it's time for Miles' nap."

Daisy thinks, *If Miles is asleep, he can't play.*
She sneaks into Miles' room . . .

. . . and gently pokes his hand
to wake him.

Waaaaah!

Miles starts to cry.

"Daisy, what are you doing in Miles' room?" asks Mom.

"Sleeping isn't fun," Daisy pouts.
"I want to play with Miles."

"Miles likes to play while we change his diaper," says Dad.

Daisy watches as
Dad rubs Miles' belly.

Pat-pat!

And Miles smiles.

He gently tickles him.

Tee-hee!

And Miles smiles.

Daisy watches as
Mom coos.

Goo-goo!

And Miles smiles.

She makes silly faces.

Honk-honk!

And Miles smiles.

"I want to try!"

So Daisy coos.
Goo-goo!
And Miles just stares.

She makes silly faces.
Honk-honk!
And Miles looks away.

She rubs his belly.
Pat-pat!
And Miles sucks his fingers.

"Maybe he'll love when
I tickle him!" shouts Daisy.

Waaaah!

"How are we doing, Daisy?" asks Mom.
"Miles won't smile for me," moans Daisy.

Daisy tries extra hard
to make Miles smile.
She sings to Miles.
La-la!

She dances.
Tippity-tappity!

She cartwheels.
Whoosh-whoosh!

Miles still doesn't smile.

Daisy has an idea.
"Mommy, can I change Miles' diaper?"

"Sure, Daisy. I'll be here
if you need my help."

"Miles, do you have a stinky diapy?" asks Daisy.
"Yes, you do-ooo!"

A yellow stream quickly wets Daisy's shirt.

Eeeww yuck!

Startled, Daisy takes a step back.

And Miles smiles.